For the gorgeous Daisy and Kirsten Walton – CC

For my lovely daughter Sophie, who makes me happy – SC

A HUTCHINSON BOOK: 0 09 176988 4

Published in Great Britain by Hutchinson
An imprint of Random House Children's Books

PRINTING HISTORY
This edition published 2002

1 3 5 7 9 10 8 6 4 2

Text © Caroline Castle 2002
Illustrations © Sam Childs 2002

RANDOM HOUSE CHILDREN'S BOOKS
61–63 Uxbridge Rd, London W5 5SA
A division of The Random House Group Ltd

RANDOM HOUSE AUSTRALIA (PTY) LTD
20 Alfred Street, Milsons Point, Sydney,
New South Wales 2061, Australia

RANDOM HOUSE NEW ZEALAND LTD
18 Poland Road, Glenfield, Auckland 10, New Zealand

RANDOM HOUSE (PTY) LTD
Endulini, 5A Jubilee Road, Parktown 2193, South Africa

THE RANDOM HOUSE GROUP Limited Reg. No. 954009
www.randomhouse.co.uk

A CIP catalogue record for this book is available from the British Library

Printed in Hong Kong by Midas Printing Ltd

Happy!

Caroline Castle & Sam Childs

HUTCHINSON

London Sydney Auckland Johannesburg

Very early one day Big Zeb got up and smiled a great big smile. 'The sun is up, the sky is blue,' she sang. 'Oh, what a beautiful morning!'

As soon as everyone was awake,
the herd set off for the water hole.
Little Zeb clip-clopped ahead.

'Feeling happy,' he sang.
'Sun up! Sky blue!
Oh, what a beauty!'

As they passed the farmer's garden Big Zeb gasped with delight. 'Oh, look,' she cried, 'all the flowers are blooming.'

Little Zeb did a happy little skip. He was looking forward to seeing his best friend, Little Hippo, who lived in the water hole.

When they arrived, Little Zeb called out, 'Little Hippo! Little Hippo! Sun up! Sky blue! Flowers all blooming. Tip top playing!'

But there was no reply. There was no glub-glub wallowing sound, as there usually was just before Little Hippo poked his head above the water. '*Not* happy,' said Little Zeb.

'Never mind,' said Big Zeb.
'He's sure to be here soon.'

Little Zeb waited

and waited

and waited.

But soon the sun was high in the sky and there was no sign of Little Hippo. 'You'll have to play on your own,' said Big Zeb.

Little Zeb was *not* happy playing on his own. Things were just not the same without Little Hippo. He trotted off into the jungle. 'Sun up! Sky blue!' he sang to try to cheer himself up.

'Oh, what a beauty,' he tried again.
There was a rustling in the bushes,
followed by a great gasp of pleasure.

'Ooo!' cried Little Piggy.
'Who me? Me, a beauty?'

Little Piggy danced around in a circle.
'Me, the beauty,' she sang.
Little Zeb wasn't sure that Little Piggy
was beautiful, but she seemed so
happy, she made Little Zeb
feel more cheerful too.

'Let's wallow!' cried Little Piggy,
and they wallowed.

'Let's jump!' cried Little Piggy,
and they jumped.

'Let's run!' cried Little Piggy,
and they ran...

and they ran
and they ran
and they ran
straight into...

Little Zeb pushed Little Piggy forward.
'Here's the beauty,' he said proudly,
'our new friend!'

'Let's wallow!' cried Little Piggy,
and they wallowed.

'Let's snuffle!'
cried Little Zeb,
and they snuffled.

Glug!

Big Zeb smiled when she saw the three babies.
'Well, you should be happy now,' she said to Little
Zeb, 'now you have *two* friends to play with.'

Little Zeb thought he would burst with joy.
'Sun up! Sky blue!' he cried.